Magical Mayhem

Part Eight

To Prevent New Allies

Emily Martha Sorensen

To Prevent New Allies

To Frederik Vendelin,

longtime fan of the comic,
reader of my other books,
and Patreon supporter.

Chapter 1
The Bribe

Flakes of snow swirled through the frigid air. Snowbelle danced through them with a total disregard for temperature.

She was a magie with snow powers, a Snowy in Tarc. To the uninitiated, that meant she was a magical girl who had been born in Snow City, Antarctica. But to a Tarcie, HA HA, being so formal would be insane! Most Tarcies' parents had come from Australia, and almost everybody here used abbreviations for things.

Snowbelle giggled as she twirled through the flurries. She wasn't quite as graceful as Fay, her friend with ice skating powers, but she enjoyed being outside just as much. When you didn't have to worry about the temperature, there was something about the crisp, clear air of the Antarctican wilderness that was appealing.

Tarc was the prettiest place in the world. It was also her home. And given that she was popular, her life was great fun in every way.

Footsteps were crunching on the snow towards her.

Raul! Snowbelle panicked.

Okay, it wasn't great fun in *every* way. Her manager kept bugging her to do the ads she'd agreed to film today. But TV ads were so boring, and her parents wouldn't let her spend the money from her sponsorships until she was eighteen, anyway!

She couldn't let Raul catch up with her. He'd make her go in.

Acting like she hadn't heard the footsteps, Snowbelle summoned a blizzard and pranced off as fast as she could go. She couldn't move as quickly as somebody in snowshoes, but maybe she could get away if she confused him about which way to go.

"Snowbelle?" a muffled voice called through the searing winds and floods of flakes.

Her ice slide! Maybe she could use that to get away! It was the fastest way to travel long distances, so she used it all the time to get people between Snow City, Ice City, and Frost City. She'd sometimes even helped magies commute to Chill City, the new one that was currently being set up!

But if she used that, Raul would know for sure that she was trying to avoid him. Then he'd lecture her about responsibility as soon as she got back home, and her parents would probably take his side like they always did, and that would be so boriiiiiiiing!

On the other hand, maybe she could claim she'd always meant to go to Ice City today to see Fay, who was an Icy, and she just hadn't heard Raul because of the sudden blizzard that had come up for no reason, certainly not because she'd summoned it. Yes! That could work! Blizzos were notoriously unpredictable, right?

Snowbelle spun and shoved her hand out, creating a torrent of flakes to crystallize into ice. Just a few more seconds, and —

"*Snowbelle?*" the voice called again. There was an edge of panic to it.

Snowbelle paused. *That's not Raul, is it?*

She didn't recognize the voice at all. Which meant it wasn't her manager here to lecture her. It was probably either a brand new magie who wanted training from the strongest magie in Tarc, or a sponsor who wanted to pay her, maybe for ads that were more interesting this time.

Frozen flakes still gusted around, perhaps because wind didn't die immediately after you summoned it. But now that it was possible to see further than her face, she could see there were three people in snowshoes standing several meters away from her, wearing thick coats and hats and scarves and still shivering. Behind them were tracks walking from Snow City.

Snowbelle felt a bit bad. She hadn't meant to make normies suffer. It was clear none of them were magies, because two of them were way too old, and the third . . . okay, the one in front could be a magie, but in that case, why hadn't she transformed?

"We're, um . . ." The brown-skinned teenage girl in the front gulped, looking nervous. "I'm Florence Atkins, and these are my parents. The mayor of Snow City said we'd find you out here."

Snowbelle snorted and rolled her eyes. She could just bet she knew how he'd said it, too. *That ranga? Yeah, she's likely causing trouble outside.*

It wasn't like she had deliberately cracked the dome that one time she and Fay had gone ice skating on it. Anyway, this was Tarc, not Moon Base. They didn't need the giant domes to keep their air in, just heat. And there were magies with heat powers who had kept things warm while the dome was being repaired. True, it was best if the dome didn't need to be repaired, but they hadn't done it on purpose. How were they supposed to have known that Delicate Frost Princess's magical ice skates could cut through a magical dome if she spun on top of it long enough?

The teenage girl in front looked more nervous than ever, perhaps because of Snowbelle's derisive snort. "So . . . um . . . we need to talk to you about something official . . ."

"No worries!" Snowbelle interrupted, grinning. "Let's go inside. You look cold."

"Yes," the one in front said with great relief.

Behind her, the two adults who were hugging each other and huddling together for warmth nodded vehemently.

It was only a few minutes' walk with snowshoes, but they looked cold enough that Snowbelle figured she should get them back sooner, so she took pity on them and summoned her ice slide and shoved them down it.

For some reason, they screamed in panic as they whooshed across a giant slide that vanished immediately behind them and appeared immediately in front of them. But in only a few seconds, they were back at the edge of Snow City, and Snowbelle hopped off with easy practice as the last of the ice disappeared.

The other three tumbled off and landed in the snow face-first.

"You have to learn to balance," Snowbelle explained. "Or else you might fall off when it vanishes. But it's an awesome way to travel, isn't it? Fay says it's heaps of fun to ice skate on!"

Groans came from the snowdrift.

Snowbelle sighed and put out her hand to help the first of them get up. They were all Merries, weren't they? Their accents sounded American. Merries had snow in their country, right? They ought to know how to handle it.

She pushed the buttons on the side of the entrance, causing the first door to open, then helped the groaning shiverers into the heatlock. All three of them breathed sighs of relief as the outer door closed and warmth flooded into the enclosed space.

The heatlock was a lot like the airlock used on Moon Base. In fact, the Tarc cities had been designed and built in preparation for the Looney colony, not that any Tarcie would ever admit that. There was a huge rivalry between the two for who should get the most government funding.

Tarcies said they had more people and it was much cheaper to build new infrastructure on Tarc than on the moon. Loonies countered that their city was the first step towards interplanetary colonization, so it was more important, plus the Tarcie cities had been around for thirty years, so they should really be self-sufficient by now.

Loonies were so annoying. It was hard to believe they were both colonies of the same Aussie government.

The inner door opened, and Snowbelle guided the three people past the entrance checkpoint and over to a conference room for official business. Technically she ought to have her manager with her, but if she went and got him, he'd remind her that she was supposed to be filming an ad right now.

Also technically, she wasn't supposed to use the conference rooms without permission from the mayor, but she'd used them so often for sponsorship discussions that she figured that rule no longer applied to her. And she'd memorized his access code from watching him type it in so many times.

The Bribe

"Okay!" Snowbelle said, flopping into a chair on one end of the table. Her silky white skirt petals billowed out and fluttered gradually downwards. "What are you here to discuss?"

The three visitors were removing hats and jackets and unwinding scarves from their necks. The teenage girl stepped forward and gingerly took a seat across from Snowbelle.

The two adults hovered near the entrance, standing there with a familiar awkward air of "I feel I have to be here to support my daughter, but I really don't have anything to add, so I'll just wait here and try to look like I'm supervising or something."

Snowbelle had seen that attitude not only from her own parents a bajillion times, but also from the parents of most of the magies she wound up training. It was annoyiiiiing.

For crying out loud, she was twelve years old. She didn't need supervision. She could take care of herself. Most magies were just fine on their own. They had magical powers nobody else did!

Except for bornies, of course. But she had never met a bornie. They didn't get invited to settle Tarc. When you needed heaps of magies to keep everyone warm so that the colonies could survive, you didn't want born mages living alongside them who might turn into villains and mess up everything.

The teenage girl put her hands on her lap and took a deep breath. "I'm trying to set up a government for magical girls."

Snowbelle stared at her blankly.

"Because it's important." The teenage girl spoke rapidly, looking very nervous. "Sometimes a magical girl goes corrupt, and there need to be laws to prevent that from happening. There also need to be protections in place to prevent bullying, and even eventually to protect magical girls from exploitation by foreign governments. We won't be able to do much about the *kamikaze* right now, for instance, but maybe in twenty years, we'd have the respected authority to . . ."

"Wow!" Snowbelle exclaimed, leaping up and slamming her hands on the table. Her petal skirts poofed out in all directions. "A government for magical girls?! It's high time someone did that! That's awesome! But why are you telling me about it?"

The brown-skinned girl looked flummoxed. "Why . . . ?"

"Oh!" Snowbelle figured it out. They wanted her to make ads for it. "Sure, that sounds fine! Of course, I'll need to check your financial records and the way you're marketing yourselves to make sure everything's done right. I won't support dishonest companies, y'know. But I'm guessing that won't be a problem, since it's by magies, for magies. This sounds so cool!"

The brown-skinned girl looked relieved. "Good. I'm gl—"

"Have you seen my other ads?" Snowbelle broke in, leaning forward eagerly. "I did this one for an ice cream that made the brand really popular, even though we live in Tarc and most people prefer hot chocolate because it's not cold! I'm supposed to be filming an ad for snow boots right now —"

Come to think of it, she probably shouldn't be mentioning that she was skipping out on an ad for some other company.

"W-well . . ." The teenage girl looked awkward. "Presidente Santos said you're one of the three most powerful magical girls in the world . . . so . . ."

"Tee hee!" Snowbelle giggled, putting her face in her hands. She loved hearing nice things about herself. "*That's* true. What else did she say about me?"

The brown-skinned girl looked hesitant. "Well . . . she mentioned that your magic involves temperature . . ."

"That's *it?*" Snowbelle was miffed. "That's lame. I also have powers of weather and beauty."

"Oh! Well, I'm sure she just forgot to mention every—"

"I mean, I'm sure you already knew about the temperature powers."

The girl seemed to be avoiding her eyes. "Er . . . yes. I'm sure I've . . . heard about you before . . ."

Snowbelle ignored the implication that the brown-skinned Merrie had not, in fact, heard about her before. It was the polite thing to do. Besides, she loved talking about herself.

"And freezing, and force-shields, and tracking, and charming, and laughing, and dancing, and —" she bragged.

"Laughing?" one of the adults broke in, looking puzzled.

The Bribe

Snowbelle burst into uproarious giggles. The other three people in the room suddenly started tittering for no reason at all.

Snowbelle abruptly stopped. So did the others.

Confusion and a bit of panic crossed all three visitors' faces.

"It's infectious," Snowbelle beamed. "Do you want to see how my charming power works?"

"No!" the woman shouted, while the man said simultaneously, "No, thank you."

Snowbelle pouted. She liked her charming power. It made people immediately dote over her. Of course, it only worked for a few minutes, and it tended to not work on the same person twice, but it was really fun.

The teenage girl sitting across the table from Snowbelle took a deep breath. "So, I'm trying to set up the Magical Girl Union. Presidente Santos told me I should recruit you . . ."

"Force-shields are fun, too! I can stop any heat-based attack!"

". . . because you're highly respected . . ."

"And tracking! I can track anyone who's walked through snow! That's really useful in Tarc, let me tell you. I've rescued missing children that way."

". . . and that's . . ."

"Well, just one, but he was a boy, so he wasn't a magie, and he was four, and his mum said I saved his life."

"Um . . ."

"Okay!" Snowbelle said, slamming her hands on the table. She leapt up, and her petal skirts swished every which way. "I'll do it! My manager will go over my usual sponsorship rates —"

"Wait, what?" The brown-skinned girl looked alarmed. "I don't think you —"

"Hey, what do you think of including my friend Fay in the first ad? You've probably heard of her. She's Delicate Frost Princess, and she has magical ice skates —"

"I'm not here to talk about commercials!" Florence shouted.

Snowbelle blinked. People didn't usually yell at her. "Then what are you here for?"

The brown-skinned girl gulped.

"Er . . . I don't think you understand," she said carefully. "I'm here because you're highly respected leader of magical girls. We want you to help run things."

Snowbelle's excitement shriveled to nothing.

"Whaaaaaaaaaaaat? Run things?" she said flatly. "I don't want to run things. That's why I have a manager."

The Merrie looked desperate. "But you're a highly respected teacher of magical girls. You'd be perfect to help run the Magical Girl Union."

"Don't wanna," Snowbelle shrugged, waving her hand. "I'll do the ads, though."

"But we need you!"

Snowbelle wasn't impressed. She'd heard begging before. She got up from the table. "You can get in contact with my manager about the ads. Happy to help there. I've gotta go film an ad for snow boots now. Excuse me."

She started to head for the door, but a bald man was standing in front of it.

"If you're not on board, the Magical Girl Union won't happen," he said quietly.

Snowbelle stared at him, puzzled. "Of course it will. Just find someone else."

"Florence was told to talk to three different magical girls," the woman said. "If all three support her idea, she'll be able to set up the Union. If even one says no, she won't."

Snowbelle was irritated. Were they trying to guilt-trip her? She'd made her decision, and it was her choice to make.

"Look, mates," she snapped, "I'm sure it's very, very important, and will probably help lots of people. So don't give up just because I'm not gonna do it. Go find somebody else! There are lots of magies out there!"

"But you just said yourself how important it is!" the teenage girl cried.

"Don't care," Snowbelle said stubbornly.

The teenage girl closed her eyes and seemed to be thinking for a long moment.

Finally, she stood up and walked over, looking Snowbelle right in the eye.

"Snowbelle," she said carefully and clearly, "to be honest, I think we need your charisma to get anything done. I haven't got it, and we need it. You're good at convincing people to buy things. You could use that skill in diplomacy, as well. I don't need just some magical girl who's respected across the world. I need *you*."

Snowbelle squirmed uncomfortably. Her parents and manager were the only ones who usually talked straight to her like that. Most people were either flattering or deferential. Even the mayor, who wasn't terribly fond of her, treated her with great care.

"But I don't want to," she scowled. Even to her own ears, her voice sounded petulant.

"You can do a lot more than just advertise things," the Merrie girl said softly. "You can change a lot of people's lives for the better. As you travel all over the world, you can convince people to do the right thing. I mean . . . 'If you believe in something, you have to use your gift. Because if you don't use it, the losses will be swift.'"

Snowbelle sucked in her breath.

It was exactly the same as one of the lyrics in the English translation of Lentswe Counterpoint's latest song. And that was seriously frustrating, because Snowbelle didn't *want* to help, but if she went against Lentswe Counterpoint's declaration of what everybody should be doing, she could never count herself as a true fan again . . .

Snowbelle marched back to the table and flopped back into her chair. She put her chin in her hands and glowered.

The teenaged Merrie looked nervous and went back to her seat. She waited, pleating her hands in front of her.

The silence was very, very uncomfortable. Snowbelle couldn't stop thinking about the song, which was now running through her head. The second verse was even more pointed than the first: *"And those who will do nothing, / I tell you you're a curse. / Because your life's accomplishments / Will just make the world worse!"*

That was so unfair! Snowbelle had never realized how unfair that verse was!

It wasn't true! She wasn't making anything worse! She was making everything better! She only supported honest companies, and she broke up rivalries, and she taught new magical girls, and she kept the weather stable during the worst storms that were about to hit all three cities, and . . .

And maybe she was helping only people in Tarc.

Maybe she needed to be helping people all over the world.

Argh! That was so unfair!

It wasn't the only thing that was unfair, either. She'd tried to buy tickets to Lentswe Counterpoint's next live concert, the one that was happening next month, but she'd gotten there too late, and the ticket scalpers had been asking such high prices for the sold-out concert that her parents had told her there was no way they would let her spend that kind of money on them. *So unfair!*

And *now* someone was quoting Lentswe Counterpoint at her, when she was about to miss a concert that she really, really wanted to go to, and . . .

Actually, come to think of it . . .

"We really need you," the teenage girl said.

Snowbelle had come to a decision. She shrugged and kept her chin in her hands, looking away. "Ehhh . . . I'll do it if you get me tickets to Lentswe Counterpoint's sold-out concert next month."

"What?" three voices chorused.

"Lentswe Counterpoint's sold-out concert," Snowbelle repeated matter-of-factly. "If you want me so much, you'll buy me concert tickets. I missed the chance to buy them myself."

The adults were muttering under their breaths. The woman looked weary, and the man looked startled.

"Counterpoint's . . .?" the girl in front of her said slowly.

Snowbelle nodded firmly.

"*I LOVE HER MUSIC!*" The girl exploded out of the chair, waving her hands excitedly.

"I know!" Snowbelle squealed. "Isn't she amazing?!"

"She doesn't even use autotune magic —"

"Right! Because she doesn't need it! Fay doesn't believe it, but it's totally true —"

"And she's super anti-apartheid, which is so cool — and, like, the duets —"

"I KNOW! The way she splits herself in half!"

"I wish I knew her secret identity," the Merrie girl chattered excitedly. "I've read so many speculations in magazines —"

"I like that she keeps it a secret," Snowbelle said, grinning. "It's part of the mystery. Besides, it doesn't matter, right? She's always saying people shouldn't wonder what race she is, because it doesn't matter. Oh, she's SO COOL!"

There was a cough from off to the side. Snowbelle turned to look at the adults, annoyed at the interruption.

The bald man looked exasperated. "Are you saying you want to be bribed into helping Florence run this new government?"

"It's not a bribe, Dad!" Florence exclaimed. "It's a Lentswe Counterpoint ticket!"

"*Three* tickets," Snowbelle said, holding up three fingers. "I want to take both of my boyfriends with me."

"You have *two* boyfriends?" Florence's mother looked appalled.

Snowbelle grinned. "Yeah, they're fighting over me. It's great."

"Aren't you *twelve?*" Florence's father objected.

"I'm very grown-up for my age."

His eyebrow twitched.

"We can buy her tickets, right?" Florence asked pleadingly. "If it's not too expensive, maybe we can buy one for me, too!"

"That'd be great!" Snowbelle said, clapping her hands. "I can tell we're going to be best mates!"

She couldn't wait to go with Florence to help convince the other two magies to help. It was the least she could do for another Lentswe Counterpoint fan.

She knew she was amazing. She could convince anybody of anything. As long as it wasn't, say, somebody like . . .

"*CHUNG-AE?!*"

Chapter 2
The Subordinate

Korea had been conquered by Japan just over ten years ago. And Japan was not a nice nation to have been conquered by.

One of the first things Emperor Kami had ordered was that all Korean people be forced to take Japanese names. Then he had eradicated their language from the schools, making it forbidden for children to speak it or read it. Officially, Korea was now part of Japan, and Korean people were considered second-class citizens.

The Korean people were still fighting back.

Not with guns or battle magic, though both had been tried initially. Whenever violent rebellion was attempted, the Japanese government took swift and bloody retribution. Instead, the Korean people now fought through stealth and information.

They fought through the Righteous Army.

Shortly after Korea had been conquered, a professor of Korean history had secretly founded the Righteous Army as an underground academic organization, working to quietly preserve his nation's language and culture despite Japan's determination to stamp them out.

His family hadn't known about it until he had been caught and executed, his wife and children executed along with him. Only his seventeen-year-old daughter had survived.

The Subordinate

Escaping with only the barest fragments of what had been a mighty underground movement, the professor's now-orphaned seventeen-year-old daughter had reached out for magic to protect herself and others.

This was Chung-Ae.

With only fragments of her father's Righteous Army remaining, Chung-Ae had rebuilt the organization in his honor from the ground up, focusing not only on the preservation of culture and history, but also on the collection and training of magical allies who could eventually liberate Korea for good.

To have become a magical girl at the very old age of seventeen was highly unusual. To still be one now, at nineteen years old, was extraordinary. And her powers showed no sign of cracking. There were whispers that she might even eventually become one of those exceptional magical girls who reached the age of thirty without losing her powers, a feat so rare that it had only ever been documented twice, both times in the country of Mali.

To still have her magic at the age of nineteen meant she had to be a woman of great virtue and wisdom. The very fact that she was still a magical girl hinted a giant implication that her cause was just, which meant Korea's plight was getting more and more attention from citizens of other countries, including the world powers of Australia, Brazil, and Germany.

The Japanese emperor profoundly hated Chung-Ae.

But she cared little what others thought of her, least of all the emperor she was supposed to obey. Her role was to protect and to facilitate, not to speak pretty words to those who wanted to feel good about themselves for agreeing with her cause while making no sacrifices for it.

Examining the map of Korea on the wall beside her usual seat at the planning table, Chung-Ae moved several of the pins to represent new conquests that had been made.

She did not personally supervise the military actions of the *uileon sonyeo,* nor did she condone the fact that some of the girls under her watch were starting to go out and pick minor fights with the *kamikaze* in order to rescue loved ones.

Still, she could not blame the fighting magical girls of the Righteous Army for their impatience. After months of training, they were finally starting to behave in an organized enough manner that hopes were running high that they might soon be able to face the *kamikaze* directly and destroy them.

Personally, Chung-Ae had no such hopes. She considered the *uileon sonyeo* a necessary last resort, not the ideal solution. The bloodless revolution of the nation of *Terra de Liberdade e Mágica* five years ago had given her hope that such a thing might also be possible in Korea. The *kamikaze* were victims of the emperor, too, after all.

For many generations now, both Japan and China had been conscripting magical girls into military service: the *kamikaze* or "divine wind" in Japan, and the *tianlong* or "heavenly dragons" in China. Originally, both country had used their magical young girls only to defend their borders. But the usefulness of their magic had eventually resulted in the military leaders thinking more creatively.

In the 1950s, the *tianlong* had driven the British government out of Hong Kong, reclaiming the land that China had lost in the Opium War.

In the 1970s, the Japanese *kamikaze* and the Russian military had clashed in a gigantic squabble over the ownership of the Kuril Islands. Unlike Japan, Russia did not require its magical girls to fight, but rather pushed them into public service. Despite this seeming disadvantage, the tsar's forces had won, perhaps because of all the *domovoi* with healing powers who were volunteering in military hospitals throughout the conflict.

In the 1990s, the *tianlong* and the *kamikaze* had kept being sent to constantly claim and reclaim a number of tiny islands in the East China Sea from each other.

For the most part, such military uses of magical girls had not been controversial, as the girls had been treated like the children or young teenagers that they were.

And then Emperor Kami had come to power in Japan.

There were many horror stories now about the *kamikaze* and how Japanese girls who gained magic were treated.

Parents were bribed with huge amounts of money if they had a daughter who became a magical girl and turned her in to the government. If they failed to do so, and a friend or neighbor did so instead, the person who reported the girl was given the reward instead, and the parents were sent to prison.

The vast majority of girls in the *kamikaze* were given regular memory wipes, courtesy of a born mage with the power to do that who Emperor Kami kept as an advisor, in order to erase any memories of battlefield incidents that might make them less innocent if they remembered them, and thus more likely to lose their powers.

There were even rumors of literal magical brainwashing in some cases, because a girl who was magically brainwashed wasn't responsible for her actions and thus wouldn't lose her powers if she did awful things, but these were only rumors, with nothing substantiated. Still, Chung-Ae had no reason to doubt that Emperor Kami would be above such a thing.

So she did not hate the *kamikaze*. Instead, she pitied them. And every time she heard about a Korean magical girl being discovered by the *kamikaze* and ripped away from her home to be forced to join them, Chung-Ae's blood boiled.

The time would come when Korea would be free. And when that time came, perhaps the magical girls of Japan would rise up against their emperor, too.

She only hoped it could be done without a bloody revolution. One thing her father had taught her as a child was that most violent revolutions only succeeded in replacing one terrible despot with another. And if the next despot was not imposed from outside but rose up from within their own nation, it would be much, much harder to convince the people that no improvements had been made.

Above all, Chung-Ae practiced patience, waiting for an opportunity with no casualties, because she wanted to make sure that freeing Korea would mean that they were actually free.

As she reflected on this, moving another pin, she heard a commotion rising up from outside the outer walls.

"But you have to let us in!" a voice was shouting in English, or perhaps German. Chung-Ae did not understand the meaning of the words, but she was familiar with the cadence.

Both languages were banned within Japan and Korea, much like Portuguese and the Korean language itself. Emperor Kami had not responded well to pressures from the three world powers to maybe stop brainwashing his country's magical girls.

Chung-Ae shook her head in exasperation. More and more magical girls from other countries had been sneaking over the Korean border to try to visit Righteous Army's headquarters over the past year. Some came with offers to help; most came to gawk. She had explained over and over again that the Righteous Army was not a tourist destination, and yet they kept on coming.

"I'm sorry. No foreigners may enter," one of the *uileon sonyeo* guards said in whatever language the foreigner was using.

"But Presidente Santos sent us!" the other voice insisted. "We're supposed to talk to Chung-Ae —"

Ah! Chung-Ae heard the name and realized what had to be going on.

She had received a letter from the President of Mágico a few days earlier saying that an emissary from her country would be coming, and to please extend that person every hospitality.

Unfortunately, Chung-Ae had been across the country, using her protective shield to rescue a group of *uileon sonyeo* who had picked a fight too large with a ridiculous number of *kamikaze,* when the letter had arrived. So she had not had the opportunity to read it immediately.

One of Chung-Ae's powers was that any letter addressed to her would teleport to her the instant it was finished. However, she could not read Portuguese, so she had tucked it into her pocket until she got back to headquarters to have it translated.

She had only read the translation of that letter a few hours ago, and had not thought to inform the guards outside the gate already. She had not expected the visitor so soon.

Chung-Ae walked briskly outside to reach the gate before the guards were successful in sending the invited emissary away.

The Subordinate

One of them, Eun, did not speak any languages other than Japanese or Korean, and her Korean was rusty because she had not been allowed to use it for most of her childhood. So she was talking vehemently in Japanese. *"Go away! This is not a place for tourists! No foreigners are allowed! Shoo! Shoo!"*

The other guard was Chin-Sun, one of the most respected of the *uileon sonyeo,* and one of the Righteous Army's most valuable spies. Chin-Sun seemed to speak every language in the world, and could surely have been scolding the visitors more effectively than Eun. She, however, was simply standing with an aloof air and her spear in a semi-threatening position, seemingly uninterested in saying any more than she had a minute earlier.

"Chin-Sun! Eun!" Chung-Ae announced, speaking in Korean. *"Grant them entrance. I have been warned of their coming."*

While Chung-Ae was, of course, fluent in Japanese, she had not spoken the language in over a year, making it a point to always speak Korean to the members of the Righteous Army, especially to those who were weak in it.

If necessary, translators could be provided to those whose Korean was nonexistent. But speaking in Japanese directly to her subordinates was a line that Chung-Ae would not cross. She was Korean, as were they, and the restoration of their language was one of the things the Righteous Army was fighting for.

Chin-Sun turned, a suspicious look on her face. *"Warned of whom? These tourists?"*

"They are not tourists. The President of Mágico has sent them. Let them in."

Chin-Sun moved aside with great reluctance.

Eun hesitated a little longer. *"Are you sure they aren't spies?"* she asked, speaking in careful Korean.

Chung-Ae nodded. *"I am sure. A description was provided of the main emissary, as well as the other two that might be with her. That one is Snowbelle, of Snow City. That one is Florence Atkins, formerly Pink Dragon. And . . ."*

Chung-Ae paused, frowning. There were four people here, and the letter had mentioned three.

The third description had been of a teenage girl with some sort of pastries attached to her head, but neither of the other two who were standing past the guards matched that description. They were a man and woman who appeared to be middle-aged.

"Who are those?" she asked at last.

"We don't know either, Chung-Ae," Eun said.

Chung-Ae shook her head, exasperated. She was not inviting anyone in whose presence she had not been forewarned about. *"They stay outside."*

Once the guests had been taken in to the meeting room and been provided with sweet rice tea, which the one named Florence tentatively sipped and the one named Snowbelle rudely wrinkled her nose at and pushed away, Chung-Ae sent for an interpreter.

The best choice, of course, was Mun-Hee, who spoke more languages than anyone else at camp. Her skill with languages put even Chin-Sun's abilities to shame. Of course, Mun-Hee's personal skill had little to do with it; she had an heirloom focus item that had belonged to four women in her family, and all of the magical girls before her had had linguistic powers.

The vestiges of the previous magical girls' powers within her focus item meant that she had exceptional prowess with languages when transformed, even though her own powers were unrelated to translating.

"Welcome to the Righteous Army," Chung-Ae said formally, seating herself as she gestured towards her interpreter. *"I am Chung-Ae. This is Mun-Hee."*

Mun-Hee, an excitable fourteen-year-old girl who was loyal, albeit a bit lazy, waved and spoke in rapid English, which was apparently the language both the visitors spoke. "Hello! Welcome! I'm Chung-Ae's interpreter, Mun-Hee!"

Assuming the girl had translated her words correctly, Chung-Ae waited expectantly for the two guests to speak.

The one named Florence did so. "Er . . . great. Well, I hope I'm not intruding on your valuable time . . ."

"Chung-Ae! Are they wasting your time?" Mun-Hee chirped.

Wondering why her visitors would start a conversation that way, Chung-Ae answered, *"Not yet, but ask them not to linger."*

Mun-Hee cheerfully interpreted this. "Chung-Ae says don't take long!"

"Gack!" Florence's eyes went wide. "Okay . . . um . . . how do I summarize . . .?"

As the visitor embarked on a long explanation in English, leaving no pauses for Mun-Hee to translate any of it, Chung-Ae reflected, as she often had before, that the fancily twisted loops of Mun-Hee's hair seemed to be held in place with no fasteners.

That hairstyle would no doubt be a nuisance to recreate, if not downright impossible, without the transformation magic that produced it perfectly for her every time.

Mun-Hee's costume could be excused from the same oversight because a similarly loose-fitting dress might be possible to slip over one's head in reality. But that lack of attention to detail in the hairstyle was awfully distracting.

Of course, that sort of omission was not rare. A magical girl's costume was part of her body, so there were no limits to how it might look, save that it could not be removed unless specifically designed for that purpose.

The English monologue finally trailed off, which meant that Mun-Hee launched into a similarly long and wandering explanation in Korean, adding in a lot of things like, *"Oh, wait, I forgot this!"* or *"Oh, yeah, she said that before this part!"*

Despite the garbled explanation, Chung-Ae caught on to the gist immediately.

"You want to prevent another situation like the kamikaze?" she asked, looking at the two visitors.

Once the words were translated, the one named Florence nodded vehemently. "Yes! Yes, that's exactly what I mean!"

Having heard the translated affirmative, Chung-Ae sat back, pleased. She knew the dangers of corrupted magical girls better than most. Those dangers were directly responsible for her nation's current situation.

"Go on," she said.

The conversation continued with much back-and-forth. Chung-Ae was very intrigued. The idea that Florence Atkins was presenting seemed quite valuable, and she was impressed by the clarity of purpose behind it.

The conversation continued with much back-and-forth. Chung-Ae was very intrigued. The idea that Florence Atkins was presenting seemed to be something of tremendous value, and she was impressed by the clarity of purpose behind it.

She was less impressed by the orange-haired Snowbelle, who started to make muttering complaints under her breath that Mun-Hee then proceeded to translate helpfully.

"'Waiting for things to get translated is boring. *Chung-Ae should learn English.' 'Gah! Don't translate what Snowbelle just said!!'* Too late."

Chung-Ae tried not to show the amusement she felt. She would not reward rudeness, though it might at times be entertaining.

In a stern tone, Chung-Ae put in, *"Rude as her words are, Snowbelle's meaning is well-taken. Asking for my involvement in Mágico seems impractical, given that we do not share a common language."*

Once this was translated, the brown-skinned Florence looked panicked. She leapt up and started talking frantically.

"But we need your support!" Mun-Hee repeated. *"We can't do it without you! Presidente Santos said —"*

"You have my support," Chung-Ae interrupted. *"What I question is your desire for my presence."*

"— doesn't think she actually needs to be there," Mun-Hee finished translating for Florence.

"But we *do* need you! You represent honor and freedom, not to mention wisdom and discipline —"

"— very smart and everyone likes you, and you're, um, what's that one pillar of Mágico, the one that isn't magic or freedom or family, the one that's sorta like age?"

"You mean wisdom?"

"Wisdom! Yes! I think that's what she means."

"What did she say after that?"

"Ummm, something about being good at getting things done, I think? I forget the rest."

Chung-Ae was seeing some definite problems in this process of translation. She was certain she had made the right decision.

"I appreciate the compliment, but I am far too busy to spend time personally attending," she said firmly. *"Mun-Hee?"*

"— does not think she needs to personally — Huh?"

"You do it," Chung-Ae ordered.

Mun-Hee looked at her blankly. *"Do what?"*

"Go to Mágico. Attend their meetings. Report back to me."

"Nonononononononononononono!" Mun-Hee leapt out of her seat in alarm. *"Chung-Ae —!"*

Chung-Ae's cheeks tightened in annoyance. *"'Anything but a combat position,' you said. Were you lying?"*

"That isn't fair!" Mun-Hee wailed. *"I never volunteered to leave Korea! I'm not like you! I still have a family!"*

"All of your family members are in the Righteous Army, and your father has done far more to aid against Japanese occupation than you. When you are the one with the magic, no less. Aren't you ashamed?"

"I'm not brave like you, Chung-Ae!" Mun-Hee burst into tears. *"Don't be so mean to me!"*

Across the table, Florence and Snowbelle were watching this exchange with great confusion on their faces.

"Mun-Hee!" Chung-Ae ordered, very irate. She pointed to the doorway. *"I am displeased. Go fetch Chin-Sun."*

Mun-Hee leapt out and ran out of the room, crying and saying something about being sorry, only she wasn't brave, and it wasn't her fault, that was just how she was, and . . .

Bravery, Chung-Ae thought with frustration, *is not something one is born with. It is a skill one practices in order to improve it. I was not brave two years ago, either.*

She heard a murmur of voices as Chin-Sun was relieved of her post at the gate. A few minutes later, Chin-Sun entered the meeting room.

She stood with a tall, sharp spear in one hand, held firmly. Those looking at her would probably assume that it was her focus item, as she carried it everywhere with her. It was not. *"Mun-Hee says you wanted to speak with me?"*

Chung-Ae sighed heavily. *"Yes. Chin-Sun, I believe I have heard you speak English?"*

"I speak twelve languages. English is one of them."

The loyal subordinate said nothing more than that, but her grip on the spear tightened, betraying the tension she was feeling.

In other words, Chin-Sun had been using her eavesdropping power to listen in on the whole conversation from her post at the gate. Given how good she was at spying, Chung-Ae could hardly be surprised, but it was a trifle exasperating to find out that one's own spies were not above intense nosiness at home.

Showing a hint of that exasperation, Chung-Ae added, *"And given your eavesdropping power, I assume you already know I need someone in Mágico for me."*

"You wish to send me away?!" Chin-Sun burst out.

It was a question that had no right answer. Chung-Ae answered honestly. *"Absolutely not. I can ill-spare you. But since we apparently cannot count on Mun-Hee . . ."*

That did not seem to make Chin-Sun any happier. *"This sounds like a demotion, Chung-Ae."*

"I know, Chin-Sun. I'm sorry. Can you recommend another member of the Righteous Army who I could trust and who can speak English?"

Chin-Sun was silent for a long moment. *"No."*

Chung-Ae sighed. She had hoped for the opposite answer. *"Then I'm afraid it has to be you. If only there were many who spoke English and were willing to admit to it, it would be different. But ever since English was added to the list of banned languages, to find someone who admits to speaking it . . ."*

"I know it's banned!" Chin-Sun exploded. *"That's why I learned it! I make it my business to learn everything Japan forbids us!"*

"Quite," Chung-Ae said, nodding. *"Which is why you are one of our finest spies. Your thirst for knowledge is insatiable."*

Chin-Sun did not seem comforted by this compliment.

A thought occurred to Chung-Ae. Slowly, she said, *"But even those skills need not go to waste in this position."*

Chin-Sun gave her an angry, hurt look. *"I fail to see how . . ."*

Chung-Ae flicked a glance over to the two English speakers. It was not impossible that one of them actually spoke Korean, but if they were that good at hiding what they knew, they were competent spies already, and would not doubt infer the contents of this conversation even without comprehending the language. In which case, she might as well speak freely.

"Come, Chin-Sun," Chung-Ae said, smiling slightly. *"We both know that allies do not always stay that way. Ten years ago, the* kamikaze *asked for our help against the* tianlong. *We gave it to them. In return, they betrayed Korea when their emperor asked them to conquer us. I believe that Eloise Santos is a leader who has integrity. But suppose she is not the President of Mágico forever? Regimes change. Motivations change. Loyalties change. Korea has been betrayed before. I ask you to please make sure that that history does not repeat."*

There was a long silence. Then Chin-Sun bowed her head. *"Of course, Chung-Ae. You are correct. Forgive my shortsightedness."*

"And I hope you will forgive mine, for ever thinking Mun-Hee would have been sufficient for this position," Chung-Ae said dryly. *"In retrospect, she would have been completely ineffective in an emergency. I will miss you badly. Yet, what you can achieve there may be of crucial importance. As long as they are allies, we will give them whatever help they need. But the instant we catch wind that they are betraying us . . ."*

Chin-Sun raised her head. A ghost of a smile gleamed across her face. *"We will crush them."*

"Precisely."

Chung-Ae flicked a glance over at the two English-speakers, who were both still staring cluelessly. It was amusing.

"You will be my ambassador," Chung-Ae said, turning back to Chin-Sun. *"You will have authority to make decisions on my behalf, so long as you do nothing too extreme. I trust both your judgment*

and your loyalty." She paused as a thought occurred to her. *"I believe you speak Portuguese?"*

"Yes. I learned it at school."

"Then that will be of great value, too. In much the way that we are speaking freely in front of them . . ." She spread her hand to indicate the two English-speakers whom she presumed did not understand Korean. *". . . so will others speak freely in front of you when they think you do not understand. You will be in a country where the principle language is Portuguese. And so, if they are not already aware that you speak Portuguese . . ."*

Chin-Sun's eyes glinted. *"I will not inform them."*

"Good. And keep your magic quiet for as long as you deem prudent, as well. They need not know what you are capable of doing. The time may come when surprise will be a valuable asset."

Her spy, one of the finest in the Righteous Army, smiled.

It wasn't that Snowbelle *hated* Chung-Ae. It was just that her mate Fay had gone to Korea on vacation last year, and she'd tried to visit the Righteous Army headquarters to see what it looked like, but the guards hadn't let her in, which was *so rude* that Snowbelle had been ticked off about it ever since.

And now Snowbelle was even more irritated. After ten minutes of the two Korean magies talking in some language that Snowbelle was guessing was Korean, but which could've been Japanese or Chinese for all she knew, the interpreter named Mun-Hee had been called back in, and she had tearfully repeated Chung-Ae's explanation that this other person called Chin-Sun would be going with them.

So in other words, not only had Chung-Ae made Florence's parents stay outside, which was bad enough already, now they were even having a lackey shoved off on them. So! Rude!

The lackey they were supposed to just accept sat on the stairs outside the meeting hall, a spear placed across her lap, surveying them with a silent and almost hostile stare.

"So you're . . . Chin . . . Sun?" Florence asked hesitantly.

The Korean girl said nothing.

"It's nice to meet you," Florence tried.

"Oh, no, it isn't!" Snowbelle broke in. "This is insulting, Florence! I hope you realize that! Chung-Ae's sticking us with her *lackey?!* She's insulting us, plain and simple! It won't do us any good to have some lackey who doesn't even speak English!"

"I do speak English," the Korean magie said coldly. "I understand every word you say. You will call me 'ambassador,' not 'lackey.'"

"Oh, good," Snowbelle said, folding her arms. "It's good to know you were just being deliberately rude by staring at us silently."

"I'm sorry!" Florence scrambled to intervene. "I'm sure she doesn't mean —"

"Too right I do!" Snowbelle yelled, talking over her. "I like you even less than Chung-Ae, mate. And whaddya mean, ambassador?! Ambassadors don't just sit there and glare. Ambassadors *talk!*"

The Korean girl simply raised her chin and said nothing.

"If you keep on acting like such a snob in front of Dulcina, I'll have to slap you!"

"Snowbelle . . ." Florence said through gritted teeth.

Realizing she may have gone too far, Snowbelle backed off a bit. "Okay, I wouldn't really do it. But seriously!"

"Who is Dulcina?" the Korean magie demanded.

Florence looked relieved about the change in subject. "She's the next magical girl whose support we need. We'll be going to visit her next."

"I see," Chin-Sun said flatly. "And who exactly is she?"

"You *haven't heard of Dulcina?*" Snowbelle burst out. "Have you been hiding under a *rock?* She's nearly as famous as me! She's *amazing!*"

Chin-Sun's lips curled up. "I've never heard of you, either."

"Then you're an idiot!"

Florence looked very weary.

Chapter 3
The Insurgent

Dulcina didn't believe in wallowing in self-pity. If she had, she would have cracked long ago.

She crept behind a grown man who was stalking two small children, his hand hovering over a knife in a sheathe by his side.

Wait for it, Dulcina thought, silently summoning her focus item, which was a long paper stick. A twist of pink sugar whirled from nowhere, whipping into cotton candy around the stick.

The two children didn't seem to notice the man after them. They were chattering and laughing, digging through a trash can for the remnants of food somebody had left there.

Many years ago, Dulcina had been just like those two, rooting through trash to find something to live on. After her parents' deaths in the crossfire of a shootout between two rival gangs, and after all of their money and property had been confiscated by a series of corrupt government officials, Dulcina had been thrown into the Mexico City Government-Run Orphanage.

It was not an institution that was interested in taking care of children. It was an institution that saw children as a burden they were legally required to begrudgingly take in and feed and clothe. After three weeks there, three-year-old Dulcina had fled in the middle of the night to live on the streets on her own.

There had been no guards posted. No one had come after her. She had discovered later that the institution saw runaways as an effective way to lower their expenses and get rid of most potential troublemakers without having to face any legal culpability.

Unlike many other runaways in similar situations, she had still had the advantage of innocence back then. Which meant that, as a girl, she'd had the option to become a *niña bruja*. So she had.

It hadn't really been intended, at first. The first time she had transformed, it had been out of hunger and desperate envy, watching a rich child's parents buy him candy in the park. She'd had a vague idea that magic was something people could do, and maybe her mother had even talked to her about it once, though she couldn't remember what had been said.

As a hungry child, the thing she'd longed for the most had been candy. And so naturally she'd wound up with candy powers. At first, she'd used those powers to feed herself. And then she'd figured out that she had no limit of how much she could create, so she'd started to share with other children.

For years, she'd detransformed whenever she wasn't actively using her magic. This had sometimes resulted in situations in which she'd woken up to find unscrupulous adults or teenagers trying to rob her or even kidnap her to use her powers for their own gain.

Finally, she'd realized that as long as she was transformed, she never grew hungry. She never needed to sleep, either. And she had no need of a double life.

So she hadn't detransformed in over a decade.

A human life was vulnerable.

Dulcina needed no vulnerabilities.

Silently, Dulcina spun her paper stick around, waiting to see what the man would do. If he was more innocent than he looked, she would show mercy. Her role was to protect the innocent, not to punish those who only appeared guilty.

In a sudden movement, the man snatched the blade from his hip and dashed towards the children, roaring ferociously.

The two children screamed and scattered.

The man bolted after them, his legs longer and faster. He was rapidly catching up.

Dulcina stood her ground and wound up her arm, cursing the criminal silently. If he had tried to be stealthy, that would be one thing. But he had actively warned the children and provoked them to flee, putting as much terror into their hearts as possible. That meant he wasn't merely a thief, acting out of desperation.

He was a bounty hunter.

Last year, one of the local crime syndicates had put a bounty on the head of any magical girl brought to them, because they were sick of *chicas brujas* interfering in their operations.

Since then, any child not accompanied by an adult in areas without police had been in terrible danger. And the police were too much in the pocket of the syndicates to ever patrol the slums.

So Dulcina had been doing it for them for years, stopping any criminals she could find and protecting the street children who seemed to be more plentiful every year.

It was illegal, so she often got shot at by any police who happened to bother to show up. She didn't much care.

She also sometimes found herself accosted by reporters or flatterers who insisted that she was so admirable, and they were so honored to meet her, and . . .

Right. If people *really* admired her actions, they should stop wasting her time and get to work helping her. But no, all of those people who considered her so brave for breaking the law were much too cowardly to do it themselves.

She hurled her stick towards the man just as he seized the child who looked more like a little girl by the arm and yelled, *"I'll kill you! I'm gonna kill you!"*

Just in case the two children he'd found didn't have magic, he was hoping to lure in another magical girl, it seemed. It was a common tactic among bounty hunters, appalling because it often worked.

Well, he'd lured in a *niña bruja* in, all right. Just the last one he'd probably hoped for.

Dulcina smiled grimly and snapped her fingers.

The Insurgent

"Cotton Candy WHIRLWIND!"

The lance of paper snapped through the man and exploded outwards into a cloud of fluffy pink sugar. The little girl was knocked flying, and Dulcina flung a giant marshmallow in that direction to catch her fall.

The child landed and started to scream deafeningly.

The man stabbed his way out of the sticky cocoon, leaping up to his feet, eyes blazing in triumph and terror.

"Dulcina Caramelo!" he yelled. *"You have the greatest bounty of all!"*

He whipped a gun out from under his shirt and shot at her. She dodged, but irritatingly, it managed to shatter one of the ice cream cones she wore in her hair.

She plucked one of the seemingly ornamental hard candies from the fringe of her blouse and expanded it into a gigantic purple shield. The next three bullets ricocheted as she yanked the sash from her waist, which was actually one very long rope of yellow and orange licorice.

The man shoved the shield aside and stabbed at her with the knife, sending her licorice rope flying. She jabbed her knee into his stomach, shoving him away and dislodging one of the gumballs from her left sandal in the same movement. She tossed in her mouth and started to chew.

The other ice cream cone shattered as she dodged another gunshot. The gum was almost soft enough to make a bubble, which she could use to trap —

Out of the corner of her eye, she caught sight of the empty sugar cocoon dissolving into the air. That meant the stick was ready to be used again. Even better.

It was her focus item, so she could summon it. The paper stick vanished from across the road and reappeared in her hand.

"Cotton Candy WHIRLWIND!" she yelled.

The man was enveloped in clouds of sticky sugar.

He yelled a threat and started to stab his way out, but Dulcina was already moving. She grabbed one of the three lollipops from her necklace, made it gigantic, and clubbed the trapped man in the head with the shiny orange disc of rock-hard candy.

The man collapsed to the ground, the cocoon wrapping itself tighter and tighter around him.

Dulcina grinned, blew a gum bubble that was three times her size, and snapped it at the man with a practiced flick of her wrist as she summoned the paper stick back into her hand. The pink bubble encased him in a binding that was flexible and yet nearly impossible to break. It also coated the knife and squished its way into the barrel of the man's gun, making both weapons completely useless.

It would have been easy to kill him. Very easy. And she frankly was tempted to do so. He would only hurt or kill more children later, after all. But she'd noticed that magical girls who killed tended to lose their powers sooner.

She was keenly aware of the fact that she was seventeen, nearly too old to keep her magic. If she did anything to cut it shorter, she would be endangering the lives of every child in this city.

Besides, the one thing Dulcina feared was having to go back to a human life again. It was the one nightmare she tried never to think of.

A whoosh of cold air exploded from behind her.

"Dulcina! Dulciiiiiiiiiiiiiiina!" a cheerful voice cried in English. "Remember me?"

Dulcina closed her eyes briefly. It was one of the admirers she tried so hard to avoid. "Must I?"

She heard an excited giggle. "You're so funny! Of course you know who I am!"

Dulcina turned and faced the Antarctican with folded arms. "Yes, I remember you, Snowbelle."

"I haven't seen you since the last time I came here to film an ad!" the orange-haired girl cried excitedly. "Speaking of which, do you want to —"

"No."

"But it would be really —"

"For the last time, I will not film any commercials with you."

"But it's perfect! It's for a brand of hot chocolate with candy cane bits in it —"

"And please learn to speak Spanish, if you must keep bothering me."

"This isn't about that! I didn't come about ads this time!" Snowbelle posed dramatically. She paused. "Although you should. But anyway. This is much, much better!"

Dulcina stared at her with narrowed eyes.

"See, there's going to be this government for magies — you call us *chicas brujas,* right, mate? See, I've learned a bit — that we're going to be in, you and me! We'll be able to make up rules and enforce them, and you just won't believe how awesome — Oh, wait, I forgot to slide them over. I told them I would as soon as I found you."

Three other people shot down the ice slide at a rapid pace, landing in a heap on top of each other.

"That one there's named Florence," Snowbelle said, pointing at one of the three strangers in the pile, Dulcina wasn't sure which. "It's her idea. Anyway . . ."

Dulcina ignored Snowbelle's endless explanation and eyed the new visitors warily as they picked themselves up, looking sore and rubbing various parts of their bodies that had landed on the broken concrete road of the slum.

Two of the strangers were middle-aged, and one looked close to the same age as Dulcina. The woman and the teenaged girl wore prominent cross necklaces, while the man wore what appeared to be a pastor's collar, which immediately irritated Dulcina, as she had seen too much hypocrisy to like religion.

Many times, religious people had come to her to express their admiration for what she was doing to help the poor. But were they ever willing to give up their comfortable lives on the right side of the law in order to help? No. When it came down to it, their personal lives were always more important to them than a cause they claimed to believe in.

Snowbelle's incessant chatter showed no signs of slowing.

"Because we both know magies can be really powerful, except just when we get all 'I know how to use my magic wisely,' then we start to lose our magic from getting too old! It's awful and it's not fair, and you must know what I mean, mate — you're seventeen, aren't you? That's pretty old for a magie, although Chung-Ae's nineteen. That complete snob that people love for no reason! I reckon they just love her because she's got this whole tragic family story, plus she's still got her powers and is nearly nineteen, which means she's pretty ancient, for a magie. Makes her seem like she's wise, or something. Which doesn't make sense! I've trained ankle biters who are just as smart as she is, and not one bit snobby. I've trained hundreds of them! I've been doing this since I was yea high — well, of course you know that, mate — and so have you, and she has no business coming in at seventeen and just taking over people's favor as a powerful magical girl. She's respected all over Asia, and she hasn't worked for it since she was tiny, like we did, so she doesn't deserve it! Not to mention this Chin-thing girl we're stuck with now, who is nobody, but for some reason Chung-Ae's making us take her with us. Just wait till you meet her. She stayed in the plane. She said she didn't care about meeting you. She's such a snob! I hate her! Anyway, so here are the plans, mate, and I think they're really great. We need to start this thingamabob to try to help out magies who don't have enough representation, but also to make sure we all get accountable for the same things. You know, stop corruption before it can be an issue, that sort of thing. Don't want magies to get too stuck up and start acting like villains, you know? I mean, no magies under me would do that, but you never know, the rest of the world might have lots of people that we just never see. I don't know about you, mate, but I'm really busy down in Snow City, and I see things sometimes that concern me. And there's Chung-Ae! Proof that stuck-up people can jump up on the scene and take over, and we can't do anything about it, because someday we'll be too old to have magic or respect or anything. I don't know about you, mate, but I want to leave behind a legacy of strength through goodness, so nobody gets all confused and starts thinking they can rule the world or something. We've got heaps of power, but we don't have any accountability! Better for the world, and everybody, if magies need to have rules just like anybody. Because rules are important, right, mate? We can make sure future generations of magies understand that, and we can build something really neat that will ensure a good time for everybody —"

"No," Dulcina interrupted.

Snowbelle's chatter skittered to a halt, as if she had tripped over her tongue. "Huh?"

"No," Dulcina repeated. "Please go away."

"Wait!" Snowbelle cried. "I'm sorry! I should've let you talk, right? I sometimes forget."

"I've noticed," Dulcina said dryly.

Snowbelle looked sheepish. "Can I explain it again?"

"If you're brief. Every moment I'm not patrolling the streets is a moment somebody might get hurt or killed."

"Okay." Snowbelle took a deep breath, and launched into a much more comprehensible and well-organized explanation at a much more coherent pace.

It seemed the thing she was excited about was a brand new government for magical girls. She explained the purpose of this new government. She explained the reasons it needed to exist. She explained the goals it was trying to achieve. She explained why Dulcina would be key in influencing other people to accept its authority. And the more Dulcina understood, the more she was filled with a growing feeling of grim disapproval.

". . . And that's why it's so amazing!" Snowbelle finished at last, leaning forward and beaming. "And you can be a key part in making it happen! What do you think?!"

Dulcina turned away. "No, thanks."

"*Whaaaaaaaaaaaaaaaaat?*" Snowbelle seemed dumbfounded. "But — but — why?!"

"I have no desire to participate. In fact, I hope that you fail."

"Wait!" The girl with the cross necklace leapt up from her seat on the ice slide. "I'm sure she just didn't explain it properly! It's basically —"

"— a system to prevent corruption by increasing accountability through the creation of a new bureaucracy?"

The girl hesitated. "Well . . . yes."

"Then you should understand why I oppose it. Bureaucracies do not decrease corruption; they just inhibit freedom. If your new union is incompetent, it will be a hindrance. If it is competent, it will be worse. If you were interested in tearing down the governments we have already, I would gladly lend my support. But to build a new one sounds appalling."

The girl was staring at her, slack-jawed. "But —"

"*Look* what I spend my whole life doing!" Dulcina snapped, gesturing at the captured man in the alley. "Do you think I could protect the homeless and forgotten if a government had any say in my top priorities?!"

The man in the bubblegum had awakened and was starting to struggle. Several children crept over, not ones he had chased, and started to run over and poke at him. Discovering he couldn't get at them despite his lunging and unintelligible threats, two brave little boys giggled and started to jump on top of him. The bubblegum made for an excellent trampoline.

Dulcina plucked a handful of hard candies off the fringe of her blouse and tossed them over. The children jumped off the man and ran to catch them, giggling and squealing with excitement. Even more children appeared from the other direction.

They had all, apparently, seen her Cotton Candy Whirlwind from a distance and bolted this way to see her. All the street children in Mexico City knew that wherever Dulcina was meant food and safety.

Her face softened, and she smiled slightly. The admiration from the people she protected was the only thing that mattered. It was moments like this that made everything worthwhile.

"I think," the girl with the cross necklace said from behind her, seemingly picking her words with care, "that we both agree the corruption of someone who has power is a bad thing. That's the whole point of this. We don't want corrupt magical girls to become a new form of tyranny."

Dulcina whirled on her, riled. "Don't you *dare* say that we are a danger to the world! We are the only people who ever bother to *save* it!"

The teenaged girl looked alarmed and took a step backwards. "But that's just what I mean! We're trusted so much right now that if anybody ever tried to seize more power than they have already —"

"We'd get a benevolent monarchy in which only the kindest keep power?" Dulcina snorted. "Where do I sign for this?"

"Don't even joke about that!"

Dulcina gave the idiot a contemptuous look. "What makes you think I was joking? Every time magical girls have risen up against a corrupt government, it has been to the people's benefit. Look at Mali, which has had peace for eighty years. Look at India, which lost its yoke of bondage to Great Britain. Look at Mágico —"

"Those were whole populations rising up against a corrupt government, *including* magical girls! It's not the same as magical girls taking over!"

Dulcina snorted. "Believe me, I would do it myself if I felt any desire to rule things. The only leader who can be trusted is one who has been proven pure through magical means."

"Ya reckon, mate?" Snowbelle said, folding her arms skeptically. "Just 'cause someone's pure doesn't mean they know how to run things." She grinned and pointed at herself. "I'd be terrible, for instance."

Florence laughed at the self-deprecation. Dulcina didn't.

"If we want peace, and an end to crime forever, someone has to rule the world," Dulcina told them seriously. Why couldn't they see the obvious? "And the only people pure enough to do it are the magical girls."

"I'm not sure that would accomplish what you think it would," the bald man put in. "Power tends to corrupt. It corrupted the original Christian Church under Constantine, even though it was the most powerful organization for good in the world at the time. Seeking after political power tends to destroy purity."

Dulcina gave him a contemptuous look.

"I wasn't talking about religion," she said with distaste. "Our magic system has far more discernment than your God does."

"Does it?" he snapped, looking very angry. "Does it really?"

"Dulcina," the woman said quickly, stepping forward, "it's okay if you have some philosophical differences of opinion. In fact, that may make your involvement more valuable. This is an opportunity to affect the way magical girls are treated on a world scale. This union is intended not only to act as a system of accountability, but also as a system of protection. It can determine what unique rights magical girls should have and make sure they're not infringed. I'm sure you want to be part of that."

Dulcina considered it. "Yes, I would be interested in protecting the rights of magical girls to rule the world."

"Magical girls have no business ruling the world!" the girl with the cross necklace exploded. "We're supposed to protect people, not seize authority!"

"Ha!" Dulcina smirked. "Visit Mágico sometime, and then tell me magical girls can't do a better job at governing than professional politicians! Eloise Santos is the best national leader the world has ever —"

"THIS WAS HER IDEA!"

Dulcina paused. "Really?"

"Yes!" The girl with the cross necklace looked exasperated. "She thinks the Magical Girl Union is important for the exact same reasons I do!"

Dulcina frowned. "That makes no sense. I naturally assumed she planned to spread her authority across the continent. If she wanted to rule the world, I'd back her."

"She believes in democracy!" The girl stared at her in disbelief. "That's why she ran for office, and didn't just try to take over the country. If she lost an election, even to the worst candidate ever, she'd accept it!"

Dulcina gave her a look of polite disbelief. "No magical girl would sit back and allow corruption to take hold."

"She would if she believed in the system. If she believed that breaking the law would just make things worse."

Dulcina's eyes narrowed. Frowning, she stared at the American with the cross necklace. She had the distinct impression that this would-be founder of the Magical Girl Union was talking more about herself than about Eloise Santos, but she couldn't be sure.

"All right," Dulcina said abruptly. "I will go with you to see Eloise Santos, and perhaps I will help you found this . . . thing. Your naiveté is annoying, but I might be willing to listen to *her* reasoning."

"YAAAAY!" Snowbelle exclaimed, bouncing over and grabbing Dulcina's shoulder. "That means we're finally in this together! I knew we'd make an awesome team!"

"We are not a team," Dulcina snapped, pushing her away.

"Sure we are!" the orange-haired Antarctican declared. "You'll need girls to cover your absence in Mexico City, right? Can't leave kids undefended while you're doing meetings with us. I made heaps of friends when I came here to film the ad, and I'm sure they'll be willing to patrol if I ask them! Let's see, there are nine girls in Mexico City, three in Tepoztlán, one in Oaxtepec, three in Lerma de Villada, those two sisters in Tlalnepantla de Baz . . ."

Dulcina's mouth fell open. Her greatest fear was that, when she lost her magic, there would be no one willing to protect those she was now defending. The only people she ever interacted with were fans or victims. Victims rarely had the power to defend each other, and fans were never willing to help when she told them to stop fawning and start helping instead.

There were other magical girls stopping crime around the city, but none of them had ever started because she'd told them to. She had thought it was impossible to ask for help and get it.

How? How could this orange-haired girl, who had only been in the city a few times for short periods, be so confident that she knew so many people who would be willing to help out?

Did she know something that Dulcina lacked?

If Dulcina learned it, would she understand how to convince an appropriate magical girl to take power and the Mexican people to rise up in a revolution to help her accomplish it?

She had always assumed that once she lost her magic, her human life would end shortly thereafter. She had no interest in a life where she was a powerless victim. Once she lost her magic, she had always planned to keep fighting until she got killed.

But perhaps there was another role she could fill. Perhaps acting within one organization would teach her how to run another. One she truly believed in. One in which her human life could be of value, and not just worthless trash.

Perhaps, if she helped to found the Magical Girl Union, she would be able to change the organization, or make one of her own, to promote her own values of magical girl superiority.

"Let's start with an ad spot!" Snowbelle exclaimed. "Everyone I know wants to see you beating a criminal on TV, so that'll be the best way to promote the Magical Girl Union ever! For the backdrop, I have this great idea —"

"I will do no commercials," Dulcina said flatly. "Ever. I mean it."

Snowbelle moaned.

And Dulcina smiled.

She had not realized until now that a situation like this was exactly what the world needed.

The world needed Dulcina to keep being of value to it.

The world needed her to learn how to lead.

Chapter 4
The Discovery

Head dropped against her chest, strands of hair hanging over her face, Chronos was dozing.

Two giggling girls were throwing snowballs at each other in the middle of a blizzard.

"Ten points!" a girl with curly white hair called, scooping up a handful of snow. "I'm winning!"

"But you're not gonna win!" the girl with orange hair yelled, waving her hand around. Flakes swirled into a ball in her hand. "I'm gonna beat you, and you're gonna join the Union!"

She flung the snowball, and the other girl kicked, slicing it in half with the blade of an ice skate.

"But it sounds so *boring!*" the girl with the ice skates cried. "I don't know why you want me to join it!"

"'Cause it's gonna be *awesome!*" The girl with orange hair stuck out her tongue and grinned. "Just wait until you find out who one of the other founders is at the opening ceremony —"

The scene changed. Now a lot of girls sitting around a long table, arguing.

"— a born mage!" a girl in a pink dress and brown hair was shouting, leaping up from her seat beside a long table. "Not for the *Magical Girl* Union!"

"My best friend was killed by a born mage . . ."

"It's an awful idea! We can't trust him!"

"You realize American born mage refugees have caused half of Mexico's crime wave?"

"Born mages are the lowest of the low!"

"I can't believe you would consider . . ."

The scene changed. Two magical girls at the same table were yelling at each other.

"— not just asking for help! Mascots can be useful, too!" the one with mouse ears insisted.

The other one sneered. "Like when?"

"They give girls powers they wouldn't have had otherwise!"

"Oh, please. Any magical girl can make up any power she wants to."

"Not and use it in another world!"

"She wouldn't have to *go* to another world if the mascot weren't begging for favors! Your argument makes no sense!"

"Well, maybe that's because you're stupid!"

"What exactly makes you such a genius?!"

The scene changed. The leader of the Righteous Army was talking to somebody in Korean. This was apparently connected, but Chronos couldn't understand a word of it.

The scene changed. Beneath a banner saying, "Magical Girl Union," two identical girls in fluffy, pale pink dresses turned a corner and nearly crashed into each other.

The first seemed freaked out and pointed at the other, while the second squealed and pulled out a piece of paper and pen and thrust them at the first one. Chronos recognized the Portuguese words for, *"biggest fan!"* That was about all she understood.

The second girl ran away, squealing loudly, turned a corner, and then transformed into an expressionless Asian that Chronos had never seen in her dreams before.

The scene changed. In a secluded room, a girl in a kimono and the Asian magical girl from the previous scene were intent over a map, discussing something in whispers in Japanese. The one in the kimono had been in many of Chronos's nightmares before.

The Discovery

The scene changed. A man that Chronos had seen in a few occasional nightmares, not very important ones, was standing on a stage, ranting into a microphone to a wide audience. He spoke in Portuguese, but there were interpreters, so she could hear the English off to the side.

"We have to attack them first, and crush them! Our mighty force of magical girls could rival even China's in strength, if we just organize them properly and teach them how to attack with unity! The Magical Girl Union will be useful for that purpose. We need to start with . . ."

The scene changed. A girl with lots of braids walked into a gigantic room with columns, trailed by three other girls who were all transformed into magical girl forms.

"I brought them, Presidente Santos," the brown-skinned girl with the braids said, stepping forward. She looked nervous. "Just as you asked. These are Snowbelle, Chin-Sun, and Dulcina Caramelo. Chin-Sun is an ambassador for Chung-Ae. Chung-Ae says she cannot attend personally, but we have her support."

"Good." The woman on what looked like a throne stood up. "Then the Magical Girl Union can begin. I'll call a press conference. Make sure your speech is ready."

This scene had several variations. In one, the girl in fluffy white with orange hair interrupted. In one, the woman on the throne was less than thrilled by the substitution for Chung-Ae. In one, the nervous girl with braids irritated the woman by saying that she didn't like her speech anymore, and could she have a few days to rewrite it?

But in all of them, the Magical Girl Union was founded.

It was a scene that Chronos had seen many times before, but always different. Always before, Avenging Angel had been the one speaking to the woman on the throne. Always before, the one founding the Union had been —

"Kendra!" Chronos gasped and jerked awake, head snapping upward.

"Yeah?" Kendra glanced over from across the room. She was putting a sandwich into the microwave. "Nightmare, I take it?"

Chronos licked her lips. She couldn't bring herself to answer.

The scene she had just barely been watching was gone. That meant it had transitioned from the future into the past. She must have been seeing quite near to the present. It was something that rarely happened in her dreams; she usually only witnessed almost-the-present when she was actively looking for it.

She hadn't recognized every magical girl in those dreams, but four had stood out to her in stark clarity.

Namikaze Tateru.

Golden Tingle Spray.

Dulcina Caramelo.

Crimson Dragon, also known as Florence.

Avenging Angel's chief lieutenants.

Two of them were now under the banner of the Magical Girl Union, as they had been in the future Chronos had prevented. The other two would be likely to follow.

The chances of Namikaze Tateru joining in the next few weeks were ninety percent. This wasn't as high as the ninety-nine percent of the Magical Girl Union under Kendra, but Chronos still wouldn't count on it not happening.

The chances of Golden Tingle Spray joining were lower: only forty percent. In most of the futures Chronos had seen with Avenging Angel, she had been easily persuaded, but it seemed Florence was going to be far less convincing. There was another bright side, too, which was that it looked like Golden Tingle Spray was likely to quit after she joined, due to differences of opinion with others in the Union about the issue of mascots.

See? Chronos thought, trying to convince herself, her heart hammering. *It's not going to be exactly the same . . .*

Something else caught her mind, and she jumped, startled.

There are futures with Tat'yana Tsvetok and Asiyah Azhaar in the Union?!

Those two were both extreme pacifists. There had been zero futures with them agreeing to follow Kendra. And yet there was a small, but existent, chance that one or both of them would join the Magical Girl Union led by Florence.

The Discovery

And — wait, hang on! Where's Crimson Dragon?!

Chronos stared at her hands in slack-jawed bafflement. How could Florence be part of the Magical Girl Union without being Crimson Dragon? How was that possible?

Half of Florence's futures showed no magical girl form at all. The other half showed a wild array of different magical girl forms with no pattern to them. Crimson Dragon was entirely gone.

What on Earth?!

"So? Tell me who the dream's about," Kendra said casually, leaning against the counter while her sandwich cooked. "I'll go defeat them as soon as I finish my lunch."

Chronos gulped. "It's . . . it's . . . it's . . ."

"Someone who'll be a challenge?" Kendra grinned. "Who?"

"The . . . the Magical Girl Union," Chronos stuttered. "The organization that you would have founded. The one you would have used to conquer the world. It's in every future now. I think it *exists!*"

The smile dropped from Kendra's face. Her face morphed rapidly from shock to horror to outrage.

"Someone's . . . taking . . . my . . . *PLACE?!*"

For just a flicker of a second, she even looked wildly jealous.

Chronos was not convinced she'd made the right decision in mentioning it.

She backpedaled quickly. "Well . . . not necessarily. I mean, its future is vague. This might even be a good thing —"

"No, soothsayer," Kendra cut her off. "This is not a good thing. This is precisely what I gave up everything to prevent."

The former magical girl's voice shook with rage.

"We have a new enemy."